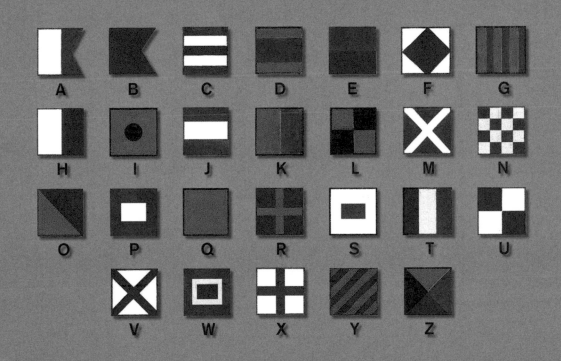

Use this signal flag chart to help decode the three messages in this book.

!

LYING AWAKE

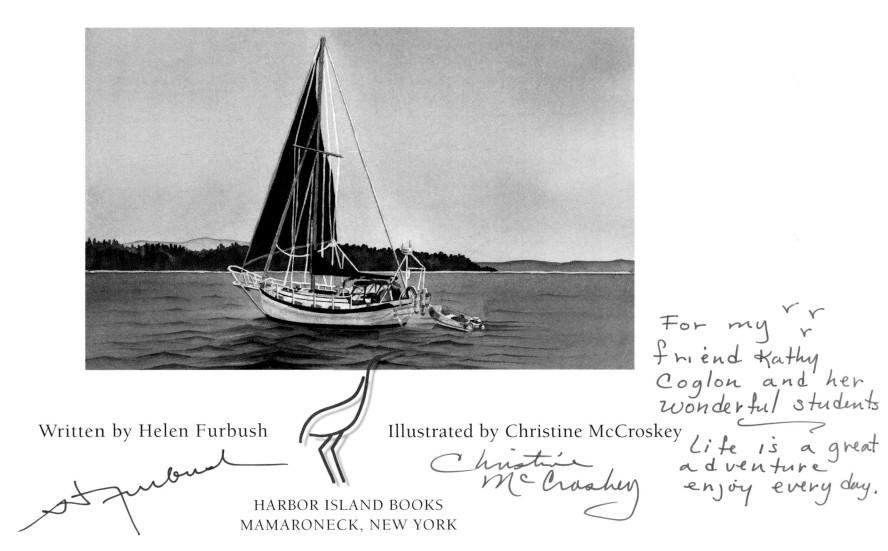

Written by Helen Furbush   Illustrated by Christine McCroskey

HARBOR ISLAND BOOKS
MAMARONECK, NEW YORK

For my
friend Kathy
Coglon and her
wonderful students

Life is a great
adventure
enjoy every day.

Christine
McCroskey

To my Lun and our four fabulous furbs: Julie, Jamie, Lauren, and Ross – Helen

Acknowledgements: to my family, especially my husband, for steadfast encouragement and patience, and to the folks who gave me feedback and support time and time again: Marlene Lee, Natalie Howard, Robin Gamrath-Schauman, Katie Mangelsdorf, my cuz Leslie Boyle, and my friends/sisters-in-law Angela Currie and Susan Holcomb. And, to my parents, Joanne and M. Staser Holcomb, for help from the very beginning. I'd also like to thank Cheryl Healy for her insightful suggestions, John Ens who invited us aboard his beautiful sailboat, the *Meretune*, to take photos and look around, and the McCroskeys for their wonderful hospitality in Roche Harbor. Finally, a salute to Chris McCroskey who proved to be more of a partner than a picture-maker.

To my husband Rich, our children Cindy and Kevin and grandchildren:
Isaac, Maddie, Katie and Lydia Rose – Chris

Acknowledgements: to my family, especially my husband Rich for his photographic skills, support and encouragement and to our daughter Cindy, son Kevin, daughter-in-law Tuvette and grandchildren for making boating an unforgettable family adventure. To my brothers and sisters for their encouragement: Nan, John, Charlotte, and Fred, and my sister-in-law Britta. To my art mentor and friend Peggy Goldsmith for her honest critique and support, and to Diane Gibbons for her critique. Special thanks to Eric Turloff for photos of his sailboat *Bajamar* and to Robert Stahl for sharing photos of his cat "Rumi." Heartfelt thanks to my MSG friends for their faith and belief in me from the start. Gratitude to Joanne Holcomb, the author's mother, who brought author and artist together. Accolades to Helen Furbush whose story, "Lying Awake," captures the joy, discovery and adventure of being with someone you love at the seashore.

Harbor Island Books, LLC
Mamaroneck, NY
www.lyingawake.net

Lying Awake
© 2004 text by Helen Furbush
© 2004 watercolors by Christine McCroskey
Printed in Singapore by Tien Wah Press

Book Design: Molly Murrah, Murrah & Company, Kirkland, WA

Library of Congress Permanent Control Number: 2003107225
Furbush, Helen.

   Lying Awake / by Helen Furbush; illustrations by Christine McCroskey
SUMMARY: An eight-year old girl lies awake waiting for sleep on Grandfather's boat, enjoying the sounds of the marina coming through the open porthole, and reflecting on the day full of adventure and discovery out on the tide flats with her grandfather.

ISBN 0-9741787-0-5

[1. Lying Awake Fiction. 2. Boats, marine life, tide flats, beach. Non fiction.]
I. McCroskey, Christine, ill. Title.

Lying awake on Grandfather's boat,
I listen to the noises of the marina.

I lie in my bunk as the boat rocks gently,
and the water slaps softly on the hull.

Through the open porthole, I hear the creak of the deck, the cry of gulls, and the groan of ropes as they strain against the pier.

I hear the chug, chug, chug of tugs and other boats passing by, and voices calling out hellos and goodnights.

And I hear the glug, glug, glug of water sloshing and gurgling under the bow of the boat.

And I think: it sounds just like the tub when you pull the plug.

From my bunk, I can smell the fresh salt air and fishy sea water. And it reminds me of the harbor seal I saw swimming in the bay, earlier in the day.

And of the great blue heron that was standing as still as a statue on the swim step of a boat across the way.

And we saw an osprey dive bomb into the water to catch a fish. He completely disappeared, and then suddenly splashed back up in the air with a fish tight in his talons.

We saw noisy crows trying to chase away an eagle perched high in a tree, and the tall black fins of orcas cruising up the Sound on their way out to sea.

And Grandfather told me: orcas usually stay together like peas in a pod.

Inside, I can barely smell the musty, dustiness of my cabin and the dim, mildewy dampness of old canvas. And I smell the fresh bed sheets that Grandfather washed, just for me, at the laundry in the marina.

And I can still smell the molasses crinkle cookies we baked after dinner, and then ate while they were warm and soft.

And I think: nothing's better than cookies baked on Grandfather's boat.

There's a faint smell of kerosene from the lantern hanging by the table, and I can see its light dancing softly on the walls of the cabin.

It looks like the sunlight that sparkled and twinkled on the tide flats, when they had stretched way out into the Sound at low tide.

Grandfather and I walked out to the very edge of the beach where the ferries, fishing boats, and barges were practically within reach.

Outside, I hear the clatter and happy chatter of a party on a boat down the dock, and I hear gulls right overhead.

And I think: gulls are always busy fussing about something.

They remind me of the gulls on the tide flats feeding on candlefish that were poking their heads out of holes in the sand.

And there were lots of pink, blue, and purple starfish, orange jellyfish, and crabs hiding under rocks and shells.

And Grandfather told me: on the sand or in the sea, let the jellies be.

And, everywhere, there were sea anemones that sprinkled water when I tickled them with my toes.

And I found a huge moon snail that was oozed all the way out of its shell. Grandfather showed me how to rub its slimy tummy until water trickled, then showered out of its body so it could get small enough to go back in.

And I think: there's always something new to find on the tide flats.

Best of all were the geoducks.

Grandfather told me: gooeys are chewy—don't put them in the pot unless they're for chowder.

At low tide, they leave big holes on the beach where they're buried in the sand. When you get too close, they shoot up jets of water to warn you away.

I loved to run over their holes to see how many fountains I could get going.

And I laughed so hard when Grandfather, bending down over a hole, got squirted right smack in the face!

Then Grandfather laughed at me when I was sprayed on my legs, and when I jumped out of the way, another geoduck got me on my back!

We waded in the freezing cold water of a deep tide channel to cross to another stretch of sand. It was so cold that I thought my feet were going to fall right off.

I didn't think I'd make it across, but I did, and after running around awhile chasing the gulls, I warmed right up.

Suddenly, Grandfather noticed that the tide was coming back in so fast, that soon it would snatch up our shoes that we'd left on some sand closer to shore.

We ran as fast as we could through pools of shells and sea grass to where they sat, alone, on a last island of sand.

What a race! Our shorts were soaking wet after all that splashing and sloshing, but we got there in time to beat the tide. We grabbed our shoes just as the water covered the sand right where they'd been sitting.

Grandfather told me: our shoes wouldn't have been the first to be taken by the tide.

Then we slowly walked back, hand in hand, across the barnacles and rocks, toward our boat in the harbor. It was time to go in and make dinner. We were going to eat out of the crab pot, and I'd never been so hungry.

Now, inside the cabin, I hear the ship's clock chime and I count the bells:

—ding ding   —ding ding   —ding ding   —ding ding

and I know it's eight o'clock.

It's too early to go to bed, but Grandfather told me: on my boat, you get up with the sun.

I hear Grandfather moving about the galley, putting the kettle on to boil, and stowing the dishes we washed after supper.

I hear him fiddle with the broken bracket on the creaky cupboard door. And, I hear him slide the griddle onto its rack, and then fasten the latch to keep it in place.

Grandfather told me: everything on a boat has to be buttoned down in case of a storm.

I hear Grandfather flick the knob of the radio to check the weather for tomorrow, then click it off again.

And I think: I'm so glad to be here.

And I hug myself, and wriggle down farther in my cozy bunk.

And I'll never forget how, a month ago, I wished harder than I'd ever wished before.

I squeezed my eyes tightly shut, held my breath, crossed my fingers, and concentrated really hard on the one thing I wanted more than anything in the whole world:

> *to be with Grandfather on his boat — just the two of us.*

I imagined myself snuggled up next to him while he played cards at the table. Then I blew and blew until the birthday candles were all blown out, and I had barely a whisper of breath left.

And a little later, like *magic*, the phone rang... and it was Grandfather!

And I think: sometimes, wishes really do come true.

Waiting for sleep, I listen again to the rap, rap, rapping of ropes on masts, and the snap, snap, snapping of sailboat flags fluttering in the wind.

I hear the clap, clap, clapping of someone's loose shutter banging on the bulkhead above the hatch.

And I hear the yap, yap, yapping of a dog on a boat somewhere in the marina.

I hear the water slap, slap, slapping against the boat, and it's saying *"hush," "hush," "hush."*

And I hear sails rustling and flap, flap, flapping and they're saying *"shush," "shush," "shush."*

Inside, I hear Grandfather playing a game of solitaire, shuffling the cards and tap, tap, tapping them on the table.

And I think: they're the nicest sounds in the world.

The ropes chiming against the masts in the marina are playing a lullaby:

"chink.....chink.....chink"

"plink.....plink.....plink"   and

"clink......clink.....clink."

And they're saying:

"time.....to.....sleep"

"go.....to.....sleep"   and

"sleep.....sleep.....sleep."

So I snuggle down to sleep,
deep under my covers,
while the boat rocks and rocks,
back and forth,
alongside the dock.

LIFE ON A BOAT

There isn't very much room on a boat, so you have to choose carefully what to bring aboard. You can only store a certain amount of food in the galley. That means you have to be well-organized, and plan all your meals in advance. When you're out at sea, you can't just run to the grocery store! But, there's always room for cookie ingredients. Cooking on a boat is fun; its smells are good company, and meals seem extra delicious. Here's the recipe for Grandfather's favorite cookies:

MOLASSES CRINKLE COOKIES

1 C sugar	2 tsp baking soda
3/4 C shortening	1/2 tsp salt
1 egg	1 tsp cinnamon
4 T molasses	1 tsp ground cloves
2 C flour	1 tsp ground ginger

Cream sugar and shortening (or butter.) Add the egg and molasses, then the spices. Sift flour and baking soda together into mixture. Chill until dough is easy to handle. Make balls (marble size) by rolling dough in the palms of your hands. Roll them in sugar sprinkled on a plate. Place on an ungreased cookie sheet. Bake 15 minutes at 350 degrees.

Two of the luxuries of being on a boat are the simplicity of life and the quietness. You're away from the hustle and bustle of life in the city and suburbs, and all its demands. On a boat, you have the gift of time. It's also a great way to enjoy nature.

Most boats don't have room for a TV, VCR, or an elaborate sound system, so you have to entertain yourself. Some of the most popular activities are reading, playing an instrument, and playing games — especially card games. Here are the rules to the solitaire game Grandfather likes to play:

SOLITAIRE

Klondike is the real name for the solitaire game most of us know. Others call it Patience, or simply, Solitaire. This game came from Canada and became popular during the 1896 Yukon gold rush.

To Set Up: Start at the left, and deal the first card face up, followed by 6 cards in the same row, face down. Return to the second card in the row, place a card on it face up, then deal 5 cards face down on the subsequent piles. Follow this pattern until you have seven piles of cards with the top card face up, each pile having one more card than the one to the left of it.

Object: To place each ace above the row of cards and build up on each by suit and in order from the 2 to the King.

To Play: Move cards on the board when playable, by placing them on each other alternating black on red, and red on black, and in descending order of value. For example, place a black 3 on a red 4, or a red jack on a black queen, and so on down. When one of your piles is topped by a card that's face down, turn it over and bring it into play. Whenever an ace becomes available, place it above your board and begin building up by suit; the 2 of that suit is next, then the 3 and so on. You may not relocate cards on the board to free up another. When a pile in the row on the board is emptied of cards, you may only place a King in that space. When there are no plays left to make on the board, take the pile of cards remaining from the set up, and turn over face up, three at a time. Make plays from the top card of your group of three, and continue through your hand pile. Work through your hand pile again and again, always in groups of three, until you can't make any more plays (game is over), or when you get down to five cards remaining in your pile. At that point, you can open up your hand and use all five. When you get that far, you might win. Have fun, and good luck!

Ropes—they're Knot Nautical!

 Although they were referred to as 'ropes' in this book, on boats they're really called 'lines.' It's not a simple matter—the rope that ties a boat to the pier is a 'line,' but other lines doing different jobs have their own names. On a sailboat, for instance, a line on the main mast that raises and lowers the sail is a 'halyard,' the one that runs from the top of the mast to the bow is a 'forestay,' and from mast to stern the line is called a 'backstay.' That's not all: a line that tows a dinghy is a 'painter,' and lines used to trim, or adjust, the sails are 'sheets.' The boomstay, headstay, mainstay, mainsheet, shroud, the jib, and a single and double stay, are all lines too. And, while we're at it, the left side of a boat is 'port', the right side is 'starboard,' the front of the boat, or bow, is 'forward,' and the back, or stern, is 'aft.' The boat's kitchen is called a 'galley,' the walls are 'bulkheads,' and the bathroom is, of course, a 'head!'

Tides and their Moon Dance

In addition to the weather, boaters also have to constantly keep track of the tides to know when it's safe to travel. Tides are caused by the gravitational pull of both the moon and the sun on Earth. The moon's pull is stronger because it's closer. The pull of the moon causes water to bulge towards it, creating a high tide. Water may rise only 2 inches at high tide, or as much as 50 feet. At the same time, water bulges at the opposite side of the planet because the moon is also pulling Earth away from the water. This means that there are two simultaneous high tides on earth, while there are also two, opposing, low tides. Every six hours there is a high tide, followed by a low tide in another six hours, and then the cycle repeats itself, roughly an hour later than the day before. When the moon and the sun are lined up together, the pull is the greatest, and tides are at their highest or lowest.

Ship's Clocks and their Bells

On a ship, bells chime on every hour and half hour to mark the time for standing watch. Watches are set up for every four hours, beginning with midnight. One bell chime sounds at 12:30 a.m. (*ding*), and a pair of chimes (*dingding*) sounds at 1:00 a.m. and so on until the end of the watch at 4:00 a.m., when eight bells will chime, in pairs. Eight bells signify the end of one watch and the beginning of the next, and so on through the day. The ship's clock chimes the same number of bells six times a day. For example, eight bells chime at 12 midnight, 4 a.m., 8 a.m., 12 noon, 4 p.m., and 8 p.m. This custom began long ago when sailors couldn't afford timekeepers, or couldn't even tell time, and yet needed to know when to stand watch. By listening to the bells, sailors could also know what time it was when it was pitch dark.

Marinas: Another Way of Life

For a fee, you can winter your boat at a marina, keep a berth year round, or just tie up for a day or two. You can use the marina's shower and toilet facilities, do your laundry, buy gas, and shop. Marina stores sell everything from groceries, swimwear, and boat supplies, to souvenirs, books and fishing tackle. There are usually restaurants nearby as well. You can hire a taxi to get into town, rent a bicycle, or explore on foot.

Of the approximately 12,000 marinas in the United States, only about 1,800 of them have facilities year round for "liveaboards." Most marinas maintain laundry and bathroom services only during the boating season. Boats are expensive to maintain, but many people find them cheaper than houses. Some folks live at the dock and go to work every day in town, while other liveaboards just want to cruise and visit the world's exotic ports.

MARINE LIFE

Harbor Seals, the Homebodies

 Harbor seals like to spend their time close to the shore, feeding on fish and squid. They rarely travel more than ten miles from their birthplace their entire life. They have the same size lungs we do, but they can hold their breath for 20 minutes. They do this by using oxygen from their blood and muscles, instead of their lungs. Seals can sleep underwater and, while sound asleep, they rise up to the surface for more air.

Blue Herons and their Bag of Tricks

When they're having a hard time catching a fish, herons will try a few tricks. One basic trick is to stand stock still with a leg poised over the water, watching and waiting. As soon as a fish comes near, they take one swift step and pounce. Sometimes they'll spread their wings to make a dark shadow over the water. Fish will hide there thinking it's a safe place from predators—big mistake. Another heron trick is to drop a small feather onto the surface of the water. When a fish comes up to investigate and take a nibble, the wily herons snap it right up.

Ospreys, the Helicopter Hawks

Ospreys are fish hawks the size of small eagles. Their wings are engineered to hover like helicopters above the water while hunting for prey. When they dive, they can completely submerge themselves, going as deep as three feet after a fish. 'Osprey' means 'bone breaker'—a very suitable name for them because of the way their powerful talons crush their prey. They build nests that weigh a half a ton, and use whatever materials are handy, like bones, shoes, old clothing, sticks or garbage. So, if you live near an osprey nest and you're missing a shoe, you know where to look!

Orcas and their Playful Appetites

 Orcas, or killer whales, are one of the fastest sea mammals on the planet (they've been clocked at 34 mph), and they're the only mammal in the world that can grow lost flesh without forming scar tissue. They're also the largest known predator of mammals; besides fish, birds and squid, their diet includes seals, sea otters, and other whales. Orcas work together, like wolves, to corner their prey. They're one of a few kinds of whales that will purposely go on land to hunt. They often use their blunt heads to break the ice where a seal or penguin is resting, and force it to jump or fall off right into their open mouths. They like to play with their food too—a couple of orcas will bat a sea lion back and forth with their tail flukes before eating it.

Bald Eagles and their Design Flaw

Eagles might look bald with their white head feathers, but that's not where their name came from—in Old English 'balde' meant white. They can see eight times better than people, and their eyes have two points of focus—forwards, and sideways. Eagles can also hear the tiniest splash from far away, and then swoop down and grab their victim without any warning. They often steal fish from other birds, such as osprey, to save themselves extra work.

Eagles' claws are their strongest weapon, but they're also their greatest weakness. First, because their claws are so curved, eagles have difficulty walking. And, second, they can't always open and close their claws whenever they want to. When they're carrying a fish, their toe tendons lock, and they can only open their claws to drop their catch if they're preparing to land at the same time. This causes problems when eagles need to drop a fish in an emergency. If, for example, an eagle grabs a lively, strong fish that pulls it down deep into the water, he can't just let go to save himself; he'll drown instead. It doesn't occur very often, but it does happen. That's one reason why eagles tend to feed on weakened, dead, or dying fish.

Moon Snails and their Tongue Drills

 When you find clam shells on the beach that have round, pea-sized holes in the center, you can bet that they were probably eaten by a moon snail. Moon snails are animals the size of a big fist that live inside a large, round spiraled shell. They have a rough, serrated tongue (a radula) to drill through shells, then scrape and suck out the animal inside. They also have an enormous foot to help drag themselves across the sand, and to capture and hold down a clam. Moon snails lay eggs in a gluey substance mixed with sand, and build a collar of eggs all around their shell. These rubber collars provide excellent protection for the eggs, which hatch in about two weeks. When you find a moon snail with its huge foot out, pick it up and rub its foot muscle firmly with one finger, back and forth. This will cause it to withdraw into its shell while showering you with its excess water. Stand back or you'll get wet!

Sea Anemones and their Paralyzing Petals

Sea anemones are colorful, flower-like creatures. When they're covered with seawater, they open up and wave all their petals, or tentacles, inviting fish to come near. When fish come too close, they use the stingers in their arms to paralyze them so they can't escape, and then they eat them. Their stingers are very effective on small fish, but they aren't harmful to humans because they can't penetrate our skin. At low tide, they close down and squat like lumpy rings of jam, waiting for the next high tide. When you touch one, they tuck in even tighter and squirt a weak spray of water in self-defense.

Starfish and their Jelly Bellies

Starfish, or sea stars, are not fish, but spiny-skinned animals with five, or as many as forty, arms. Sea stars can grow new arms if one breaks off, but it takes about a year. They can move six inches a minute, and feed on clams and mussels. Here's what happens: a starfish crawls up to a clam and wraps itself completely around it. It then injects a fluid into the clam to make it relax the strong muscle holding its two shells together. Then, with its hundreds of suction-tube feet, the starfish pulls and pulls on the shells until the clam gets tired. This could take hours. As soon as there's even the tiniest crack though, the starfish's bag-like stomach oozes inside out through its mouth, invades the clam, and slimes it.

Jellyfish, the Ocean's Drifters

Jellyfish can swim, but they rarely do. Instead, they let the ocean's waves, currents, and tides take them along wherever they go. They can only move themselves vertically, not horizontally, so they don't attack their prey—they just drift into it, or it comes to them. There are over 2,000 species of jellyfish—ranging from the size of a pea to one that weighs a ton. They all sting, but most don't cause serious injury to humans. Some, in fact, are quite harmless. When wet—in the water or washed ashore—their tentacled stingers are still active, so it's better not to touch them at any time. These beautiful sea creatures come in practically every color of the rainbow, and they're made of 95% water, 4% salt, and 1% protein.

Barnacles and their Retractable Roofs

Barnacles are tiny shrimp-like creatures that live in small white shells formed by six overlapping plates and a four-piece dome roof. At low tide, the top is tightly closed, sealing moisture in and air out. During high tide, they lie on their backs inside the shell, and stick their hairy, netlike legs out the top opening to filter food from the water as it flows by. After hatching, barnacles swim for a brief time. Then they cement themselves to something solid like a rock, shell, piling, or sea animal, and remain there for the rest of their lives.

Geoducks and their Geysers

 Geoducks (pronounced gooey ducks) are unofficially designated the state mollusk of Washington. They are the largest clam in the world, and can measure more than 8" across. Like all clams, they have a long two-holed tube, or neck, that reaches up to the surface from where they live deep in the sand. One tube of their neck is used to take in seawater for air and food. The other hole is to get rid of garbage, sewage, and excess water. When geoducks feel vibrations in the sand from something passing by, their reflex is to shoot a strong jet of spray from their garbage hole at whatever's there. They can live to be over 100 years old—the oldest found lived 146 years! They dig 1 to 3 feet down, extend their necks as long as 39 inches to the surface to eat and poop, and hunker down for the long haul.

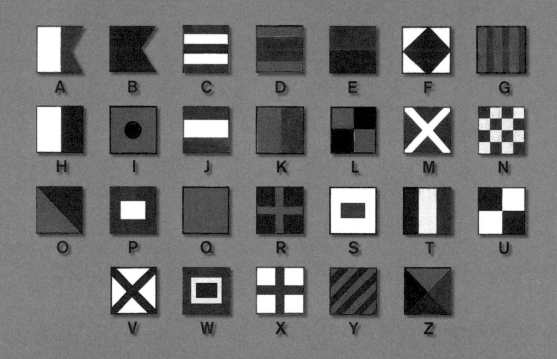

Use this signal flag chart to help decode the three messages in this book.